CLASSICS Illustrated®

Charles Dickens
A TALE OF TWO CITIES

essay by
Stuart Christie
The Dickens Project
University of California at Santa Cruz

ACCLAIM BOOKS
STUDY GUIDE

A Tale of Two Cities

Adaption by Evelyn Goodman
art by Joe Orlando

Classics Illustrated: A Tale of Two Cities © Twin Circle Publishing Co.,
a division of Frawley Enterprises; licensed to First Classics, Inc.
All new material and compilation © 1996 by Acclaim Books, Inc.

Dale-Chall R.L.: 8.35

ISBN 1-57840-003-1

Classics Illustrated® is a registered trademark
of the Frawley Corporation.

Acclaim Books, New York, NY
Printed in the United States

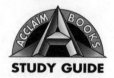

STUDY GUIDE

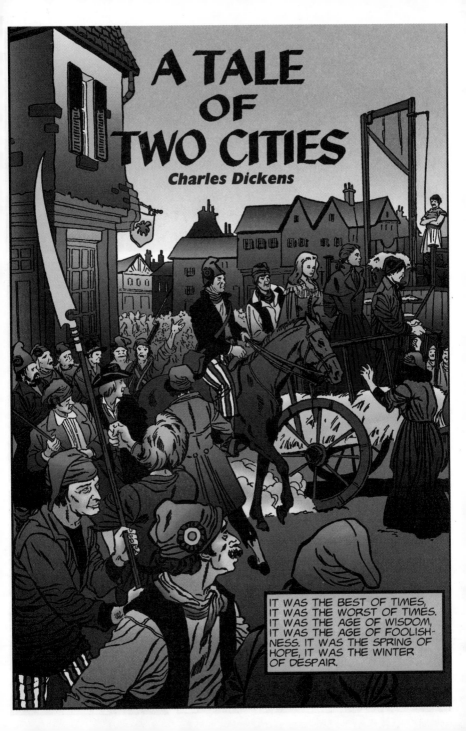

LATE IN THE MONTH OF NOVEMBER, 1775, A MAIL COACH MADE ITS WAY ALONG THE DARK AND PERILOUS ROAD FROM LONDON TO DOVER.

SUDDENLY, THERE WAS THE SOUND OF A HORSE COMING OUT OF THE DARKNESS.

HO, THERE! STOP OR I FIRE!

IS THIS THE DOVER MAIL?

WHY DO YOU WANT TO KNOW?

I WANT TO SPEAK TO A PASSENGER -- MR. JARVIS LORRY.

WHO WANTS ME? IS IT JERRY?

MISS MANETTE, TWENTY YEARS AGO, WHILE WORKING IN THE PARIS OFFICE OF TELLSON'S BANK, I HANDLED THE AFFAIRS OF DR. ALEXANDRE MANETTE.

MY DEAD FATHER!

WHEN I WAS LEFT AN ORPHAN AFTER MY MOTHER DIED, SURVIVING MY FATHER ONLY TWO YEARS, WAS IT YOU WHO BROUGHT ME TO ENGLAND?

YES, AND SINCE THEN YOU HAVE BEEN THE WARD OF TELLSON'S BANK.

NOW WE HAVE DISCOVERED THAT YOUR FATHER IS ALIVE. FOR THE LAST EIGHTEEN YEARS, HE WAS A PRISONER IN THE BASTILLE.

MY FATHER! ALIVE! WHERE IS HE NOW?

HE IS IN PARIS, AT THE HOUSE OF A FORMER SERVANT.

WE MUST GO TO HIM AT ONCE. I TO IDENTIFY HIM, YOU, TO RESTORE HIM TO HEALTH.

DR. MANETTE WAS AT THE HOME OF ERNEST DEFARGE, OWNER OF A WINESHOP IN THE PARIS SUBURB OF SAINT ANTOINE. WHEN MR. LORRY AND LUCIE ARRIVED...

WE WISH TO SEE MONSIEUR DEFARGE.

I AM MADAME DE-FARGE. MY HUSBAND WILL BE HERE SOON.

WHEN DEFARGE ENTERED ...

I WILL TAKE YOU TO DR. MANETTE. I FEAR YOU WILL FIND HIM GREATLY CHANGED.

AT THE DOOR OF DR. MANETTE'S ROOM ...

THE DOOR IS LOCKED?

HE HAS LIVED SO LONG LOCKED UP THAT HE WOULD BE FRIGHTENED IF IT WERE LEFT OPEN.

THEN ...

DO YOU RECOGNIZE HIM?

YES, BUT HOW HE HAS CHANGED!

HE WAS A SHOEMAKER IN PRISON. HE KNOWS NOTHING ELSE. HE HAS FORGOTTEN HIS NAME, AND CALLS HIMSELF BY HIS CELL NUMBER. LISTEN.

WHAT IS YOUR NAME?

105, NORTH TOWER.

WHEN DR. MANETTE SAW LUCIE. . .

WHO ARE YOU?

AT ANOTHER TIME YOU SHALL KNOW. NOW I PRAY YOU TO TOUCH ME AND TO BLESS ME.

YOUR AGONY IS OVER. I HAVE COME TO TAKE YOU TO ENGLAND TO BE AT PEACE AND AT REST.

A FEW DAYS LATER, DR. MANETTE, LUCIE AND MR. LORRY SAILED FOR ENGLAND. AS THEY BOARDED THE SHIP. . .

MAY I HELP YOU?

THANK YOU SO MUCH.

LATER. . .

YOU WERE VERY KIND TO MY FATHER. WHAT IS YOUR NAME?

CHARLES DARNAY.

DO YOU LIVE IN LONDON, MR. DARNAY?

I AM FRENCH BY BIRTH. BUSINESS FORCES ME TO TRAVEL FREQUENTLY BETWEEN PARIS AND LONDON.

PERHAPS I WILL SEE YOU IN LONDON SOME DAY.

PERHAPS.

FIVE YEARS PASSED. IN LONDON, IN 1780, DR. MANETTE, NOW RESTORED TO HEALTH, AND LUCIE WERE SUMMONED AS WITNESSES AT A TRIAL FOR TREASON. THE DEFENDANT WAS CHARLES DARNAY. LUCIE WAS QUESTIONED BY THE ATTORNEY GENERAL.

DID YOU SEE THE DEFENDANT ON A BOAT CROSSING FROM FRANCE TO ENGLAND IN NOVEMBER, 1775?

YES, HE WAS VERY KIND TO ME THEN, AND I HOPE I DO NOT HARM HIM TODAY.

THE DEFENDANT THAT NIGHT WAS CARRYING MESSAGES THAT WERE TREASONOUS TO OUR KING.

THEN DARNAY'S LAWYER SPOKE.

THE DEFENDENT THAT NIGHT WAS TRAVELING ON PERSONAL MATTERS.

ANOTHER WITNESS SAID HE HAD SEEN DARNAY COLLECTING INFORMATION NEAR A GARRISON.

ARE YOU SURE IT WAS DARNAY?

YES.

LOOK UPON MY ASSISTANT THERE. DOES HE NOT RESEMBLE DARNAY?

THE ASSISTANT, SYDNEY CARTON, REMOVED HIS WIG.

THE RESEMBLANCE IS REMARKABLE!

NOW CAN YOU BE SURE IT WAS THE PRISONER YOU SAW? OR WAS IT SOMEONE RESEMBLING HIM?

WELL, I . . . ER . . .

THE WITNESS' TESTIMONY WAS SMASHED. SOON AFTER, THE JURY WENT OUT TO CONSIDER ITS VERDICT.

AN HOUR AND ONE-HALF LATER . . .

WE FIND THE DEFENDANT NOT GUILTY.

LATER...

MR. DARNAY, WE CONGRATULATE YOU ON YOUR ESCAPE FROM DEATH.

WHEN EVERYONE ELSE LEFT, SYDNEY CARTON APPROACHED DARNAY.

LET ME SHOW YOU THE NEAREST TAVERN AT WHICH TO DINE.

IN A FEW MOMENTS...

I HARDLY SEEM TO BELONG TO THIS WORLD AGAIN.

AS FOR ME, THE GREATEST DESIRE I HAVE IS TO FORGET I BELONG TO IT. I CARE FOR NO MAN ON EARTH AND NO MAN ON EARTH CARES FOR ME.

IT IS MUCH TO BE REGRETTED. YOU MIGHT HAVE USED YOUR TALENTS BETTER.

WHEN DARNAY LEFT, CARTON STAYED ON TO FINISH HIS BOTTLE OF WINE.

DARNAY NOW SPENT MORE TIME IN LONDON, MUCH OF IT WITH THE MANETTES. BUT HE STILL MADE TRIPS TO FRANCE. THERE, THE NOBLES WERE ENRICHING THEIR POWER AND THEIR POCKETS, WHILE AMONG THE PEOPLE, HUNGER WAS WRITTEN ON EVERY FACE.

IN SAINT ANTOINE ONE DAY, A CASK OF WINE WAS DROPPED AND BROKEN OUTSIDE OF DEFARGE'S WINE SHOP.

THE STARVING PEOPLE RUSHED TO LICK UP THE WINE AS IT TRICKLED THROUGH THE COBBLESTONES.

SUDDENLY, THE CARRIAGE OF THE MARQUIS SAINT EVREMONDE CAME RACING DOWN THE NARROW STREET.

THE HORSES KNOCKED DOWN A SMALL CHILD STANDING IN THEIR WAY.

SHORTLY AFTER THE MARQUIS RETURNED TO HIS CHATEAU, SERVANTS ANNOUNCED THE ARRIVAL OF HIS NEPHEW, CHARLES -- KNOWN IN ENGLAND AS CHARLES DARNEY.

I BELIEVE YOUR NAME TO BE MORE DETESTED THAN ANY NAME IN FRANCE.

IT IS YOUR NAME, AS WELL. AS THE SON OF MY DEAD TWIN BROTHER, YOU ARE MY HEIR.

I RENOUNCE YOUR NAME! I RENOUNCE YOUR PROPERTY! IF IT WERE MINE TOMORROW, I WOULD RENOUNCE IT AND LIVE OTHERWISE AND ELSEWHERE.

SUDDENLY...

WHAT IS THAT SHADOW? OPEN THE BLINDS!

THERE IS NOTHING HERE.

THEN I AM FATIGUED AND MUST SAY GOOD NIGHT. REMEMBER, CHARLES, THE MORE THE PEOPLE HATE US, THE MORE HONORED IS OUR FAMILY.

THAT NIGHT, AS THE MARQUIS SLEPT...

THE FATHER OF THE DEAD CHILD HAD HIS REVENGE.

DRIVE HIM FAST TO HIS TOMB!

DURING THE FOLLOWING YEAR, CHARLES DARNAY ESTABLISHED HIMSELF IN LONDON AS A TUTOR. ONE DAY...

DR. MANETTE, I LOVE YOUR DAUGHTER.

I DOUBT IT NOT.

I WISH TO MARRY HER.

IF LUCIE SHOULD TELL ME YOU ARE ESSENTIAL TO HER PERFECT HAPPINESS, I WILL GIVE HER TO YOU.

THERE ARE TWO THINGS I MUST TELL YOU -- MY TRUE NAME AND WHY I AM IN ENGLAND.

WAIT! IF YOU MUST, TELL ME ON THE DAY OF YOUR WEDDING, NOT BEFORE.

DARNAY BEGAN TO COURT LUCIE. SHE LOVED HIM AS MUCH AS HE LOVED HER.

ONE DAY, LUCIE WAS VISITED BY SYDNEY CARTON, WHO HAD BEEN A FREQUENT GUEST AT THE MANETTE HOME.

I KNOW YOU CAN HAVE NO TENDERNESS FOR ME. I ASK FOR NONE. MY LIFE IS WASTED.

CAN YOU NOT CHANGE IT?

IT IS TOO LATE FOR THAT. I SHALL NEVER BE BETTER THAN I AM. I SHALL SINK LOWER AND BE WORSE--A WASTED DRUNKEN CREATURE.

CAN I NOT SAVE YOU, MR. CARTON?

NO. ALL YOU CAN EVER DO FOR ME IS DONE. YOU HAVE BEEN THE LAST DREAM OF MY SOUL.

FOR YOU, AND FOR ANY DEAR TO YOU, I WOULD DO ANYTHING. I WOULD GIVE MY LIFE TO KEEP A LIFE YOU LOVE BESIDE YOU.

THE DAY FINALLY CAME WHEN LUCIE AND CHARLES DARNAY WERE TO BE MARRIED. THAT MORNING . . .

I TOLD YOU I WOULD GIVE YOU MY TRUE NAME AND THE REASON I AM IN ENGLAND. I AM THE MARQUIS SAINT EVREMONDE . . .

NO!

WHAT IS WRONG, SIR?

NOTHING, NOTHING. GO ON.

I DESPISE MY INHERITED RIGHTS. I HAVE LEFT MY FAMILY PROPERTY IN THE CHARGE OF A SERVANT WITH ORDERS TO PLAGUE THE PEOPLE NO LONGER.

CHARLES, PROMISE ME YOU WILL NEVER TELL ANYONE ELSE YOUR TRUE IDENTITY.

IF YOU WISH, I PROMISE.

AND THAT DAY, LUCIE AND DARNAY WERE MARRIED.

THE YEARS PASSED. IN FRANCE, CONDITIONS GREW WORSE. THERE WAS TALK OF REVOLT.

IT IS A LONG TIME COMING.

WHEN IT IS READY, IT WILL COME.

IN ENGLAND, DARNAY AND HIS WIFE LIVED HAPPILY. A DAUGHTER, LUCIE, WAS BORN, AND GREW.

NICE OF YOU TO VISIT, CARTON.

I CAME TO SEE MY LITTLE LUCIE.

THEN CAME THE EVE OF JULY 14, 1789.

I FEEL AN UNEASINESS IN THE AIR.

PERHAPS IT IS THE STORM.

NO, I FEEL IT, TOO. THERE IS A FOREBODING OF SOME GREAT, AWFUL EVENT.

THE FOLLOWING DAY, A TREMENDOUS ROAR ROSE FROM THE THROAT OF SAINT ANTOINE. THE TIME HAD COME!

AT DEFARGE'S WINE SHOP...

SEPARATE AND PUT YOURSELVES AT THE HEAD OF AS MANY PATRIOTS AS YOU CAN.

WHAT DO YOU DO, MY WIFE?

TODAY, I PUT DOWN MY KNITTING AND TAKE UP THIS AXE.

I SHALL LEAD THE WOMEN. WE CAN KILL AS WELL AS THE MEN.

COME, THEN! PATRIOTS AND FRIENDS, WE ARE READY! TO THE BASTILLE!

SOON...

THEY SURRENDER! THEY SURRENDER!

IN A COURTYARD, DEFARGE SEIZED ONE OF THE BASTILLE GUARDS.

SHOW ME TO THE CELL, 105, NORTH TOWER.

THERE...

PASS THAT TORCH SLOWLY ALONG THE WALLS.

A FEW MOMENTS LATER...

A.M.! THE INITIALS OF DR. ALEXANDRE MANETTE!

HE FOUND A CROWBAR AND...

THESE ARE THE PAPERS I WANT!

THE FRENCH REVOLUTION, ONCE BEGUN, RAGED ON TO THE TERROR AND WONDER OF THE WORLD. THREE YEARS PASSED. IN AUGUST, 1792, AT TELLSON'S BANK IN LONDON . . .

BUT, MR. LORRY, MUST YOU GO TO PARIS? THE GUILLOTINE IS HARD AT WORK.

MY DEAR CHARLES, I MUST GO AND ATTEND TO CERTAIN MATTERS FOR THE BANK. PARIS IS SAFE ENOUGH FOR ME. IT IS THE FRENCH EMIGRANTS WHO ARE IN DANGER OF LOSING THEIR HEADS.

BY THE WAY, HERE IS A LETTER SMUGGLED FROM FRANCE THAT I HAVE BEEN ASKED TO DELIVER TO AN EMIGRANT. HOWEVER, I DON'T KNOW WHO THE PERSON IS.

LET ME SEE IT.

To the Marquis St. Evremonde In care of Tellson's Bank London, England

LET ME DELIVER THE LETTER FOR YOU. I KNOW THE FELLOW.

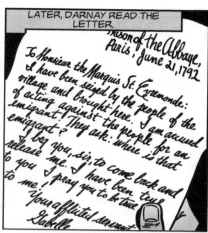

LATER, DARNAY READ THE LETTER.

Prison of the Abbaye, Paris, June 21, 1792

To Monsieur the Marquis St. Evremonde: I have been seized by the people of the village and brought here. I am accused of acting against the people for an emigrant! They ask: where is that emigrant?

I beg you, sir, to come back and release me. I have been true to you. I pray you to be true to me!

Your afflicted servant, Gabelle

I SHOULD NOT HAVE LEFT POOR GABELLE TO HANDLE MY ESTATE ALONE. I HAVE NEGLECTED MY DUTIES IN FRANCE. I MUST GO TO PARIS.

THAT NIGHT, DARNAY WROTE LETTERS OF EXPLANATION TO LUCIE AND DR. MANETTE.

THEN HE BEGAN HIS JOURNEY.

HE WAS STOPPED ALONG THE ROAD TO PARIS.

EMIGRANT, I AM GOING TO SEND YOU ON TO PARIS UNDER AN ESCORT.

IN PARIS, HE WAS TAKEN BEFORE AN OFFICER OF THE PEOPLE.

ARE YOU THE EMIGRANT EVREMONDE?

I AM NO EMIGRANT. AND I AM NOW IN FRANCE OF MY OWN FREE WILL.

YOU WILL BE SENT TO THE PRISON OF LA FORCE.

UNDER WHAT LAW AND FOR WHAT OFFENSE?

WE HAVE NEW LAWS AND NEW OFFENSES SINCE YOU WERE HERE.

BUT HAVE I NOT THE RIGHT TO...

EMIGRANTS HAVE NO RIGHTS!

A FEW DAYS LATER, AS MR. LORRY WORKED IN TELLSON'S OFFICE IN PARIS, THE DOOR BURST OPEN.

LUCIE! DR. MANETTE! WHAT HAS HAPPENED? WHAT HAS BROUGHT YOU HERE?

CHARLES IS HERE! AN ERRAND OF GENEROSITY BROUGHT HIM HERE UNKNOWN TO US. HE HAS BEEN SENT TO LA FORCE PRISON!

CALM YOURSELF, LUCIE. WE SHALL FIND HIM. I HAVE BEEN A BASTILLE PRISONER, AND THERE IS NO PATRIOT IN PARIS WHO WOULD NOT WELCOME ME WITH OPEN ARMS.

IF YOU REALLY HAVE THE POWER YOU THINK YOU HAVE, MAKE YOURSELF KNOWN TO THESE DEVILS AND GET TAKEN TO LA FORCE.

I WILL GO. LUCIE, I BEG YOU TO REMAIN HERE WITH THE CHILD AND OUR FAITHFUL FRIEND, MISS PROSS. YOU MUST NOT STIR OUT.

THE FOLLOWING NIGHT, THEY WERE VISITED BY THE DEGFARGES.

I COME FROM DR. MANETTE. I HAVE A NOTE FOR HIS DAUGHTER FROM HER HUSBAND.

MADAME DEFARGE STARED COLDLY AT LUCIE AND MISS PROSS. THEN . . .

IS THIS EVREMONDE'S CHILD?

YES.

Dearest: Take Courage I am well and your father has influence around me. You cannot answer this.
Charles

COME, DEFARGE. I HAVE SEEN THEM. WE MAY GO.

LATER. . .

THAT DREADFUL WOMAN SEEMS TO THROW A SHADOW ON ME AND ALL MY HOPES.

FOUR DAYS PASSED BEFORE DR. MANETTE RETURNED. DURING THAT TIME THERE WAS AN ATTACK UPON THE PRISONS. MOBS KILLED 1,100 DEFENSELESS PRISONERS.

WHEN DR. MANETTE RETURNED...

I WAS TAKEN BEFORE A SELF-APPOINTED COURT SITTING AT LA FORCE. I TOLD THEM WHO I WAS. DEFARGE CONFIRMED MY IDENTITY.

THEN...

MY SON-IN-LAW IS A PRISONER HERE. I BEG YOU FOR HIS LIFE AND LIBERTY.

WE WILL NOT RELEASE HIM. BUT WE WILL KEEP HIM IN SAFE CUSTODY.

I STAYED WITH CHARLES THESE FEW DAYS TO BE SURE NOTHING WOULD HAPPEN TO HIM. I BELIEVE HE IS SAFE FOR NOW.

FIFTEEN MONTHS PASSED. DURING THAT TIME, LUCIE WAS NEVER SURE, FROM HOUR TO HOUR, BUT THAT THE GUILLOTINE WOULD STRIKE OFF HER HUSBAND'S HEAD THE NEXT DAY.

FINALLY, CHARLES DARNAY WAS BROUGHT TO TRIAL. THAT DAY, FIFTEEN PRISONERS HAD ALREADY BEEN TRIED. ALL WERE CONDEMNED.

THE TRIAL BEGAN.

YOU ARE ACCUSED OF BEING AN EMIGRANT UNDER THE DECREE WHICH BANISHES ALL EMIGRANTS ON PAIN OF DEATH.

IS IT NOT TRUE THAT YOU HAVE LIVED FOR MANY YEARS IN ENGLAND?

IT IS TRUE.

VOLUNTARILY I RELINQUISHED A TITLE THAT WAS DISTASTEFUL TO ME, TO LIVE BY MY OWN INDUSTRY IN ENGLAND, RATHER THAN LIVE ON THE INDUSTRY OF THE OVERLADEN PEOPLE OF FRANCE.

BUT DID YOU NOT MARRY IN ENGLAND?

I MARRIED A CITIZEN OF FRANCE, LUCIE MANETTE, DAUGHTER OF DR. ALEXANDRE MANETTE.

WHY DID YOU NOT RETURN TO FRANCE SOONER?

BECAUSE I HAD NO MEANS OF SUPPORT IN FRANCE, WHEREAS IN ENGLAND I LIVED BY BEING A TUTOR OF FRENCH.

WHY DID YOU RETURN TO FRANCE WHEN YOU DID?

I RETURNED BECAUSE OF THE PLEA OF A FORMER SERVANT, GABELLE, WHOSE LIFE WAS ENDANGERED BY MY ABSENCE.

THEN GABELLE, WHO WAS FREED WHEN DARNAY RETURNED TO FRANCE, TESTIFIED.

IT IS TRUE. I BEGGED MONSIEUR TO RETURN TO SAVE ME.

THE NEXT WITNESS WAS DR. MANETTE.

THE ACCUSED WAS THE FIRST FRIEND I HAD UPON MY RELEASE FROM THE BASTILLE. HE HAS REMAINED DEVOTED TO MY DAUGHTER AND TO ME IN OUR EXILE.

A SHOUT ROSE FROM THE JURY.

WE HAVE HEARD ENOUGH. WE ARE READY TO VOTE.

EVERY VOTE WAS IN DARNAY'S FAVOR.

I DECLARE YOU FREE.

AND THE MOB CARRIED HIM HOME IN TRIUMPH.

DARNAY WAS REUNITED WITH HIS FAMILY.

I AM HOME! I AM SAFE!

I CAN NEVER THANK YOU ENOUGH. NO OTHER MAN COULD HAVE DONE WHAT YOU HAVE DONE FOR ME.

OH, FATHER.

DEAR CHILD, DON'T TREMBLE SO. I HAVE SAVED HIM.

BUT THAT EVENING, THERE WAS A KNOCK UPON THE DOOR.

WHAT CAN THIS BE? HIDE CHARLES! SAVE HIM!

I HAVE SAVED HIM. LET ME GO TO THE DOOR.

WE COME TO ARREST THE CITIZEN EVREMONDE, CALLED DARNAY.

TELL ME HOW AND WHY I AM AGAIN A PRISONER.

YOU HAVE BEEN ACCUSED AND DENOUNCED BY THE SECTION OF SAINT ANTOINE.

WILL YOU TELL ME WHO DENOUNCED HIM?

CITIZEN AND CITIZENESS DEFARGE -- AND ONE OTHER.

WHAT OTHER?

DO *YOU* ASK, CITIZEN DOCTOR?

YES.

THEN, YOU WILL BE ANSWERED AT THE TRIAL TOMORROW.

MEANWHILE, UNKNOWN TO ANYONE EXCEPT MR. LORRY, SYDNEY CARTON HAD ARRIVED IN PARIS. THAT NIGHT...

I HAVE BAD NEWS. DARNAY HAS BEEN ARRESTED AGAIN.

BUT I LEFT HIM SAFE AND FREE WITHIN THESE TWO HOURS!

I LEARNED OF HIS ARREST FROM A PRISON SPY WHOSE FRIENDSHIP I HAVE GAINED.

CAN THIS MAN HELP US?

NOT MUCH. BUT IF THE TRIAL SHOULD GO ILL WITH DARNAY, I CAN GET TO HIS CELL.

CARTON SPENT THE REST OF THE NIGHT WANDERING THE DARK STREETS OF PARIS, HIS MIND FILLED WITH THOUGHTS OF LUCIE AND HER CHILD.

THEN HE STOPPED AT A CHEMIST'S SHOP AND MADE A PURCHASE.

BREATHING THIS WILL MAKE ONE UNCONSCIOUS.

I KNOW.

THE FOLLOWING MORNING, DARNAY WAS AGAIN BROUGHT TO TRIAL. THE PUBLIC PROSECUTOR SPOKE.

CHARLES EVREMONDE, YOU ARE A DENOUNCED ENEMY OF THE REPUBLIC, ONE OF A FAMILY OF TYRANTS CONDEMNED TO DIE.

WHO HAD DENOUNCED THE ACCUSED?

ERNEST DEFARGE.

WHO ELSE?

THERESE DEFARGE, HIS WIFE.

AND ONE OTHER. ALEXANDRE MANETTE, PHYSICIAN.

PALE AND TREMBLING, DR. MANETTE ROSE.

I INDIGNANTLY PROTEST TO YOU THAT THIS IS A FORGERY AND A FRAUD. WHO AND WHERE IS THE FALSE CONSPIRATOR WHO SAYS THAT I DENOUNCE THE HUSBAND OF MY CHILD?

LISTEN TO WHAT IS TO FOLLOW. IN THE MEANTIME, BE SILENT.

THEN DEFARGE STOOD BEFORE THE COURT.

INFORM THE COURT OF WHAT YOU DID THE DAY THE BASTILLE WAS STORMED.

I WENT TO THE CELL KNOWN AS 105, NORTH TOWER, WHERE DR. MANETTE HAD BEEN CONFINED FOR EIGHTEEN YEARS. THERE I DISCOVERED PAPERS WRITTEN BY HIM.

LET THE PAPERS BE READ.

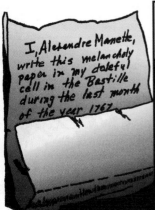

I, Alexandre Manette, write this melancholy paper in my doleful cell in the Bastille during the last month of the year 1767

"I WRITE THE TRUTH OF MY CAPTIVITY HERE. I PRAY SOME PITYING HAND WILL FIND THIS WHEN I AND MY SORROWS ARE DUST."

"ONE CLOUDY NIGHT, IN DECEMBER, 1757, AS I WALKED ALONG THE SEINE RIVER, A CARRIAGE CAME TOWARD ME."

"THE YOUNG MEN INSIDE WERE OBVIOUSLY TWIN BROTHERS."

ARE YOU DR. MANETTE?

YES.

WILL YOU PLEASE ENTER THE CARRIAGE?

"THEY DROVE ME TO A SOLITARY HOUSE ALONG A COUNTRY ROAD."

"WHEN THE SERVANT OPENED THE DOOR . . ."

DOG, WHY DID IT TAKE YOU SO LONG?

"THEN THE OTHER BROTHER STRUCK THE SERVANT IN THE SAME WAY."

THEY ARE INDEED TWINS.

"I WAS TAKEN TO A ROOM WHERE A WOMAN OF GREAT BEAUTY LAY."

MY HUSBAND, MY FATHER, AND MY BROTHER.

THERE IS LITTLE I CAN DO. SHE HAS A BRAIN FEVER.

THERE IS ANOTHER PATIENT.

"IN A LOFT OVER THE STABLE WAS THE SICK WOMAN'S YOUNG BROTHER. HE WAS DYING OF A SWORD WOUND."

THE PEASANT! HE IS HONORED! HE WILL DIE BY MY BROTHER'S SWORD -- LIKE A GENTLEMAN!

"THE BOY TOLD ME HIS STORY."

WE WERE TENANTS OF THE MARQUIS. WE WERE TAXED WITHOUT MERCY. WE WORKED WITHOUT PAY. WE WERE ROBBED AND HUNTED AND MADE POOR.

THEY WORKED MY SISTER'S HUSBAND SO CRUELLY THAT HE DIED. THEN THEY TOOK MY SISTER TO THE CHATEAU.

MY FATHER DIED OF GRIEF. I CAME HERE TO SAVE MY SISTER. NOW I DIE TOO.

MARQUIS, IN THE DAYS WHEN ALL OF THESE CRIMES ARE TO BE ANSWERED FOR, I SUMMON YOU AND YOUR DESCENDANTS TO ANSWER FOR THEM!

"THE BOY DIED IN MY ARMS. SHORTLY AFTERWARD, HIS SISTER DIED, ALSO."

"WHEN I FINALLY RETURNED TO MY HOME, I WROTE TO THE MINISTER OF JUSTICE ABOUT WHAT HAD HAPPENED. THE MARQUIS HAD INFLUENCE AT COURT. HE FOUND OUT ABOUT THE LETTER."

"AS I LEFT MY HOUSE ONE NIGHT, A MUFFLER WAS DRAWN OVER MY FACE AND I WAS BROUGHT HERE, TO MY LIVING GRAVE."

"I HAVE DISCOVERED THE NAME OF THE MARQUIS AND HIS BROTHER TO BE EVREMONDE."

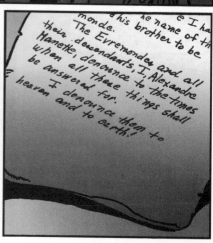

e I ha ...he name of th... ...d his brother to be ...monde.
The Evremondes and all their descendants, I, Alexandre Manette, denounce to the times When all these things shall be answered for. I denounce them to heaven and to earth.

WHEN THE DOCUMENT WAS READ, A CRY FOR BLOOD AROSE.

TO THE GUILLOTINE!

TRY TO SAVE YOUR SON-IN-LAW NOW, DR. MANETTE!

AT EVERY JURYMAN'S VOTE, THERE WAS A ROAR FROM THE MOB.

GUILTY!

GUILTY!

GUILTY!

THEN...

CHARLES EVREMONDE, CALLED DARNAY, YOU ARE BY DESCENT AN ARISTOCRAT, AN OPPRESSOR OF THE PEOPLE, A MEMBER OF A CURSED RACE. YOU WILL DIE WITHIN TWENTY-FOUR HOURS.

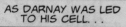

AS DARNAY WAS LED TO HIS CELL...

FAREWELL, DEAR DARLING OF MY SOUL. WE SHALL MEET AGAIN, WHERE THE WEARY ARE AT REST.

I BEG YOUR FORGIVENESS.

NO! WHAT HAVE YOU DONE THAT YOU SHOULD KNEEL TO ME? I NOW KNOW WHAT YOU UNDERWENT WHEN YOU DISCOVERED MY NAME. WITH ALL MY HEART I THANK YOU FOR WHAT YOU HAVE DONE FOR ME THESE MANY YEARS.

LATER, SYDNEY CARTON JOINED DR. MANETTE AND MR. LORRY.

YOU HAD GREAT INFLUENCE WITH THE JUDGES YESTERDAY. TRY THEM AGAIN.

YES, I WILL GO TO THE PROSECUTOR AND THE JUDGES.

WHEN HE LEFT...

I HAVE NO HOPE.

A FEW MINUTES LATER, CARTON LEFT.

DON'T GRIEVE, MR. LORRY. ALL WILL BE WELL.

CARTON MADE HIS WAY TO THE DEFARGES' WINE SHOP.

HOW LIKE EVREMONDE HE LOOKS!

THE PEOPLE IN THE WINE SHOP IGNORED CARTON.

THEY ALL MUST BE EXTERMINATED! TO THE END OF THE RACE!

BUT THE DOCTOR HAS SUFFERED SO!

I CARE NOT FOR THE DOCTOR, BUT HIS DAUGHTER --AND THE CHILD-- THEY, TOO, ARE EVREMONDES.

WE MUST STOP SOMEWHERE.

DEFARGE, THAT PEASANT FAMILY SO INJURED BY THE EVREMONDES WAS MY FAMILY. THAT BOY WAS MY BROTHER, THAT WOMAN WAS MY SISTER, THAT FATHER WAS MY FATHER.

THOSE DEAD ARE MY DEAD, AND THAT SUMMONS TO ANSWER FOR THOSE THINGS DESCENDS TO ME!

TELL WIND AND FIRE WHERE TO STOP, BUT DON'T TELL ME!

LATE THAT EVENING, CARTON WENT TO MR. LORRY'S ROOM. WHEN DR. MANETTE ENTERED. . .

WHERE IS MY BENCH? I CANNOT FIND IT. I MUST FINISH THOSE SHOES.

THE SHOCK WAS TOO MUCH FOR HIM. HIS MIND IS GONE. THERE IS NO HOPE FOR CHARLES NOW.

MR. LORRY, YOU MUST TAKE DR. MANETTE, LUCIE AND THE CHILD BACK TO LONDON AT ONCE. THEY ARE IN GRAVE DANGER HERE.

MADAME DEFARGE PLANS TO DENOUNCE THEM TO COURT. UNTIL SHE DOES, THEY HAVE CERTIFICATES PERMITTING THEM TO LEAVE THE CITY. YOU MUST LEAVE WITH THEM TOMORROW.

HERE IS MY CERTIFICATE. HOLD IT FOR ME. MEET ME OUTSIDE THE GATES OF THE PRISON TOMORROW AT TWO O'CLOCK IN THE AFTERNOON. THE MOMENT I COME TO YOU, TAKE ME IN AND WE SHALL ALL DRIVE AWAY.

PROMISE ME THAT NOTHING WILL INFLUENCE YOU TO CHANGE YOUR MIND. YOU MUST DRIVE AWAY WHEN MY PLACE IS FILLED. SEVERAL LIVES DEPEND ON IT!

I WILL DO MY PART FAITHFULLY.

AT THE SAME TIME...

TODAY, EVREMONDE GOES TO THE GUILLOTINE. HIS WIFE AND CHILD MUST FOLLOW HIM.

HOW WILL YOU GET THE EVIDENCE TO DENOUNCE THEM?

IT IS A CRIME TO MOURN FOR A VICTIM OF THE GUILLOTINE.

AND THE PUNISHMENT IS DEATH!

SHE WILL NOW BE AT HOME AWAITING THE MOMENT OF HIS DEATH. SHE WILL BE MOURNING AND GRIEVING. I WILL GO TO HER.

IN PLANNING THEIR ESCAPE, MR. LORRY HAD DECIDED THAT MISS PROSS, WHO WAS IN NO DANGER, COULD TRAVEL IN A LATER COACH. SHE WAS ALONE IN THE DESERTED ROOMS WHEN...

WHERE IS THE WIFE OF EVRE-MONDE?

IF SHE DISCOVERS THEY HAVE FLED, SHE WILL HAVE THEM PURSUED AND BROUGHT BACK.

THESE ROOMS ARE EMPTY! ARE THEY IN THE ROOM BEHIND YOU?

YOU WILL NEVER GET ME AWAY FROM THIS DOOR TO FIND OUT.

MADAME DEFARGE REACHED FOR HER PISTOL.

MISS PROSS STRUCK AT IT. THERE WAS A FLASH.

SHE'S DEAD!

A FEW MOMENTS LATER, MISS PROSS ENTERED A COACH AND WAS ON HER WAY OUT OF PARIS.

MEANWHILE, MR. LORRY'S COACH WAS LEAVING THE CITY.

HAVE YOU YOUR CERTIFICATES?

YES.

DR. ALEXANDRE MANETTE. HIS DAUGHTER, LUCIE. A CHILD, LUCIE. MR. LORRY, BANKER. SYDNEY CARTON, AN ENGLISHMAN. -- MR. CARTON IS NOT WELL?

HE WILL SOON RECOVER.

YOU CAN DEPART, CITIZENS.

AND THE COACH, WITH CHARLES DARNAY IN HIS WIFE'S ARMS, ROLLED ON TO FREEDOM AND SAFETY.

AT THE SAME TIME, SYDNEY CARTON WAS ON HIS WAY TO THE GUILLOTINE.

YOU ARE NOT EVREMONDE!

SHH!

ARE YOU DYING FOR HIM?

FOR HIS WIFE AND CHILD.

THEY SAID OF HIM, THAT NIGHT, THAT HIS WAS THE MOST PEACEFUL FACE EVER BEHELD UPON THAT PLATFORM.

IT IS A FAR, FAR BETTER THING THAT I DO, THAN I HAVE EVER DONE: IT IS A FAR, FAR BETTER REST THAT I GO TO, THAN I HAVE EVER KNOWN.

THE END

A TALE OF TWO CITIES
CHARLES DICKENS

In contrast with his later success as a world-famous author, Charles Dickens (born 1812) did not have an easy childhood. A modest but comfortable upbringing (including private school and tutors) was threatened by his family's ongoing financial problems and his father's spendthrift habits. At age twelve, young Charles was withdrawn from his schooling (his family could no longer pay the tuition) and sent to work in a blacking factory, where child labor was used to remove labels from bottles of polish and varnish, slap new labels on, and sort different colors of ink, papers, and glue for industrial use. Long hours (often twelve to fourteen hours a day) were repaid with only six shillings a week.

As represented in Dickens's novels *Oliver Twist* and *David Copperfield*, his early working years in urban London were not happy ones. To make matters worse, Dickens's father was arrested for non-payment of debts and, along with Dickens's mother and all of his siblings, thrown into the Marshalsea Debtors Prison in 1823-24. Charles found lodgings so that he could continue his work at the blacking factory. Alone, young Dickens knew that he had been educated for better things. Many of his works, including *A Tale of Two*

Cities, bear the emotional scars of these early experiences. Dominating or weak and ineffectual fathers, unjust conditions for the urban poor (particularly children), and a lasting preoccupation with imprisonment are all typical of his work.

Yet for the young Dickens, possessed of remarkable determination and the resolution not to repeat the mistakes of his early impoverished years, things improved dramatically. His parents were able to put him back into school, which led in 1827 eventually to what was in the Victorian period called "meaningful employment," first as a copying-clerk in a law office and then as a reporter covering debates in the British Parliament.

Dickens was fast and accurate as a parliamentary reporter (among the fastest in London it was said at the time) but increasingly he put his creative energies to better use. He started writing short pieces and articles for newspapers, in many cases basing them loosely upon his own experiences. In 1836 he began his first novel, *The Pickwick Papers*, in serial format. A "serialized" novel meant that 12,000 word portions of the book (usually three or four chapters in length) were published in monthly installments or "numbers" at a cheap cost. In this way, a full-length book became—spread across 19 months—more affordable for more readers.

The *Pickwick Papers* struck gold, and Dickens's future as the best-known writer of the English novel was guaranteed.

Between 1836 and 1859, Dickens wrote and published twelve full-length novels in serial format, founded two highly successful magazines, made a very successful lecture tour to the United States, and had ten children. Yet, by 1859, changes had occurred in Dickens's personal life that would have a profound impact upon his writing, including *A Tale of Two Cities,* which first appeared in serial form in November 1859.

Written towards the end of Charles Dickens's illustrious career, *A Tale of Two Cities* came at the height of his popularity and reputation in England and America. Yet 1859, the year the novel was published, brought with it profound changes for the celebrated author.

It marked Dickens's formal separation from his wife, to whom he had been married for 23 years; their relationship, by all accounts, had not been a satisfying one.

Similarly, Dickens's long-standing relationship with his publishers came to a close, and with it his role as editor-in-chief of *Household Words*, a magazine he had founded and had edited since 1850.

Though Dickens would find female companionship elsewhere, and did shortly begin publishing a second magazine (*All the Year Round*), the years just preceding the publication of *A Tale of Two Cities* were challenging ones. *A Tale of Two Cities* compares individual struggles with social revolution, and it appears that in 1858-1859 Dickens had survived a 'private' revolution of his own. After 1859, Dickens was, biographies suggest, a new man.

A TALE ON STAGE

Dickens loved the theatre and regularly attended stage productions. Wilkie Collins's *The Frozen Deep* inspired Dickens in the writing of *A Tale of Two Cities*, and the two men were friends and collaborators in a series of theatre-related efforts. In 1858, Dickens played the role of Richard Wardour in *The Frozen Deep*, a play about a doomed arctic explorer who gives his life for the man he had rivaled in love. The character of Wardour in turn inspired the figure of Sydney Carton in *A Tale of Two Cities*. Speaking of the character of Carton in a possible stage adaptation of the novel, Dickens imagined himself playing the lead: "I have a faint idea sometimes, that if I had acted him. . . I could have done something with his life and death."

A Tale of Two Cities was adapted to the stage and fulfilled Dickens's dramatic inclinations by achieving a "lasting triumph" in the English theatre. Adapted under the title *The Only Way, A Tale of Two Cities* thrilled English audiences for over a generation after Dickens's death.

Ultimately, Dickens's status as the most popular writer of his generation created pressures, not only upon his pocketbook but upon his health. He had popularized some of his earliest work—including the immensely popular *A Christmas Carol* in 1843—by performing public readings on the stage, and his love for drama never diminished. In 1858 he had helped his good friend Wilkie Collins by performing a key role in Collins's play *The Frozen Deep*, a play that most critics believe inspired *A Tale of Two Cities*.

In August through October of 1858, Dickens gave an extensive lecture tour in England, Scotland, and Ireland. In all, he gave eighty-eight readings from his works in little more than ninety days. Dickens's love of public performance guaranteed a growing audience for his novels but also contributed to his fragile health. He died in 1870, universally acknowledged as the finest novelist in the English language.

in European history, the French Revolution sent shock waves through the political and social order of Europe for over a generation. "The best of times, the worst of times"—the French Revolution remained vividly alive in the memories of the generation preceding Charles Dickens's.

Still, why did Dickens choose that revolution, rather than the English Civil War (1642-1650), or even our American Revolution? Part of the answer to the question lies in the traditional and long-standing fascination English society has had with French history and culture. (Recall that it was a French-Norman monarch, William the Conqueror, who defeated the Anglo-Saxon king and placed himself on the English throne in 1066.). Both cultures continue to share a complicated and intertwined relationship in European history as friends and allies, as well as—in the period described in *A Tale of Two Cities*—outright enemies and fierce competitors.

"It has greatly moved and excited me in the doing, and Heaven knows I have done my best and believed in it" wrote Dickens after finishing *A Tale of Two Cities* in 1859.

Part of what made *A Tale of Two Cities* so "moving" and "exciting" for Dickens and for thousands of his readers at that time was its hard look at revolution as an idea. The revolution Dickens focuses on in *A Tale of Two Cities* is the French Revolution, (1789-1794), which began on 14 July 1789 with the storming of the French prison, the Bastille, in the capital of France, Paris. A momentous event

WITH A ROAR THAT SOUNDED AS IF ALL THE BREATH IN FRANCE HAD BEEN SHAPED INTO IT, THE MOB, ARMED WITH HUNGER AND REVENGE, ROSE AND FLOWED INTO THE CITY. ALARM BELLS RINGING, DRUMS BEATING, THE ATTACK ON THE BASTILLE BEGAN

In the 1850s, France was of interest to the British for several reasons. For one thing, in 1859 England possessed one valuable item the French didn't: relative peace. No major revolution, no conflict between king and parliament, had occurred in England for almost two hundred years. It seemed to the English reader that democratic England had experienced centuries of the same social and political scene, of business as usual.

For their part, the French monarchs kept their kingdom together through force of custom and force of arms. If Britain had, to some extent, earned her peace, France *imposed* peace—at swordspoint. Up until 1789, the French kings (called the Bourbon dynasty) exercised absolute and tyrannical authority; they had outlawed the French parliaments (*parlements*) for over 150 years. If repression justified rebellion, France had missed an ideal opportunity in her Revolution against out-of-touch and self-centered rulers. Despite initial hope and tremendous possibilities for political change, France's revolution became a tragedy. Writing *Tale* in 1859, Dickens might have had these feelings in mind as he sat down to write what was destined to be among the most popular of his novels.

The French Revolution of 1789 was relatively recent history, but there had also been a series of even more recent upheavals and uprisings in each of the major European capitals—*except* London—throughout the fall and winter of 1848. Anxiety-provoking in the very least, the "Revolutions of 1848" seemed inescapable for everyone except the British. Yet to the adult Dickens, it seemed just a matter of time before the winds of social and political upheaval on the European continent would blow across the English Channel and make some profound impact upon the "island" of English culture and society. Accordingly, *A Tale of Two Cities* is Dickens's attempt to reflect upon the causes and consequences, problems and pitfalls, of social and political revolution as they appeared from his perspective: not only the French Revolution, but *any* revolution.

Dickens, like most educated, middle-class men of his day, had traveled to post-Revolution Paris, France's great capital of culture. As a tourist, he had met Victor Hugo, the popular French novelist of *The Hunchback of Notre Dame* fame (writing novels at roughly the same time, Dickens and Hugo are often compared with one another). Before beginning *A Tale of Two Cities*, Dickens did extensive research, reading French romantic philosophy, consulting studies of eighteenth-century Paris (including tax tables!), and re-reading the classic accounts of the French Revolution by English writers, notably the great nineteenth-century social historian Thomas Carlyle, whom Dickens acknowledges in his "Preface." Clearly interested in his topic, Dickens was careful to get all of the necessary initial research done before turning to write his novel.

Having completed his study, Dickens perceived that the French Revolution was a complicated series of events. In general, the events in *A Tale of Two Cities* conform to a "two-phase" account of the French Revolution. In phase one, the Revolution involved the aristocracy taking power from the monarchy.

In phase two of the Revolution, lower and middle-class French people took control of the Revolution from the aristocracy. *A Tale of Two Cities* shows the ugliness and disillusionment caused by widespread violence and unrest when, by most historical accounts, the French revolution got out of control and "devoured its own children."

Examples of how the Revolution motivated and transformed specific characters in the novel are suggested by the violent opinions and death of the Marquis Saint Evremonde as well as the vengefulness and ultimate fate of Madame DeFarge.

Dickens's writing of the novel, in serial, took a little under a year. Interestingly, for all of the punch the story packs historically, the novel is one of Dickens's shortest. In general, readers of *A Tale of Two Cities* responded enthusiastically. For English readers, the novel delicately balanced the issue of British

AND THE MOB CARRIED HIM HOME IN TRIUMPH.

distance *from*, and fascination *with*, France. As doubles and mirror-images of one another, Sidney Carton and Charles Darnay embody this split between England and France (even as the split is, ultimately, resolved). In this way, English readers of *A Tale of Two Cities* could experience the thrill, sensation, and dire atmosphere of revolution *as entertainment*, while safely reading one of Dickens's serial installments by the fireside. With Dickens as master storyteller, a public story—of violent mobs, executions, and street-level protests—is transformed into a private experience.

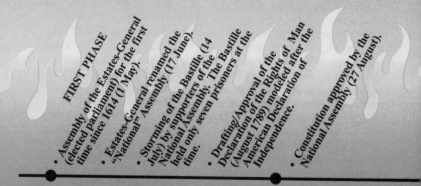

A TIMELINE OF THE REVOLUTION

FIRST PHASE
- Assembly of the Estates-General (elected parliament for the first time since 1614 (1 May).
- Estates-General renamed the "National" Assembly (17 June).
- Storming of the Bastille (14 July) by supporters of the National Assembly. The Bastille held only seven prisoners at the time.
- Drafting/Approval of the Declaration of the Rights of Man (August 1789) modeled after the American Declaration of Independence.
- Constitution approved by the National Assembly (27 August).

1789

1791

A final note about the context of the novel is important: in 1859 Dickens was banking upon his immense popularity as a writer to keep his new magazine, *All the Year Round*, afloat. With this aim in mind, Dickens took the risky step of deciding to publish *A Tale of Two Cities* in weekly, rather than his usual monthly, installments. He would have to write *A Tale of Two Cities* at a very fast pace, a process he described as "incessant condensation." His strategy seems to have worked. Encouraged by the early and immediate success of *A Tale of Two Cities, All the Year Round* sold even better than his previous magazine had, and back issues of the new magazine containing portions of *A Tale of Two Cities* were in heavy demand. Because of its broad historical scope, with much of the action occurring outside of England, as well as its terse style, *A Tale of Two Cities* is often referred to as the "least Dickensian of all of his novels". For his own part, Dickens believed *A Tale of Two Cities* to be "the best story I have written".

The Cast of Major Characters

If *A Tale of Two Cities* is often called the "least Dickensian of all his novels," a closer look at the characters in the novel proves otherwise. Each one is carefully crafted to play his or her role in a complex plot that furthers Dickens's overall design and purpose. Believable and "realistic," Dickens's characters and descriptions also possess tremendous imaginative, even fantastical, qualities: gargoyles shape-shift, coffins pursue little boys, a shoemaker's bench is murdered, thunder and rainstorms foreshadow terrible events to come, dead people rise from the grave, and live people walk the streets of night in the sleep of death. Dickens's overall style balances level-headed detail with a fanciful unsettling imagination.

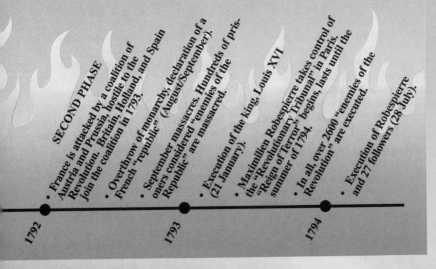

SECOND PHASE

- France is attacked by a coalition of Austria and Prussia, hostile to the Revolution. Britain, Holland, and Spain join the coalition in 1793.

- Overthrow of monarchy; declaration of a French "republic" (August/September).

- September massacres. Hundreds of prisoners considered "enemies of the Republic" are massacred.

- Execution of the king, Louis XVI (21 January).

- Maximilien Robespierre takes control of the "Revolutionary Tribunal" in Paris. the "Reign of Terror" begins, lasts until the summer of 1794.

- In all, over 2600 "enemies of the Revolution" are executed.

- Execution of Robespierre and 27 followers (28 July).

1792   1793   1794

Lucie Manette: The daughter of Dr. Manette, French-born yet raised in England, Lucie is the novel's romantic heroine. Like so many of Dickens's heroines she is pretty, sweet, and appears unaffected by the events that unfold around her, except as the primary focus of the novel's sentiment. Lucie's gaze "[knits] itself into an expression that was not quite one of perplexity, or wonder, or alarm, or merely of a bright fixed attention, though it included all the four expressions." As this description suggests, Lucie possesses just about any outward appearance one might desire. Before Dr. Manette is freed from the Bastille, Lucie believes herself an orphan, and her goal in the course of the *Tale* is to find a home. Before she can do so, however, she must undergo a purifying trial by suffering.

As both daughter and ideal love object, Lucie is Dr. Manette's only source of inspiration and hope during his many years imprisonment in the Bastille. Loved by both Darnay and Carton, Lucie represents the ultimate romantic value for both of the men. It is for her that Darnay stakes his claim and hopes for a new future against the decadent aristocratic order that his uncle—the Marquis Saint Evremonde—represents. It is for her love that Carton gives his life. Dickens writes:

> *Ever busily winding the golden thread that bound them all together, weaving the service of her happy influence through the tissue of all of their lives, and making it predominate nowhere, Lucie heard in the echoes of years none but friendly and soothing sounds.*

Dr. Manette: Dr. Manette's history drives the plot of *A Tale of Two Cities* from the beginning. It is he who, as the good father figure in the tale, both makes events happen (he is freed from the Bastille to begin the novel, and his fame among the revolutionary "Jacques" frees Darnay) and is overwhelmed by events he cannot control. In one of the most celebrated of the novel's plot twists, Dr. Manette's handwritten account of the cruelty of Darnay's father and uncle is introduced by Defarge as state's evidence against Darnay at his second trial. Tragically, Dr. Manette becomes the unwitting accuser of his own son-in-law.

Dr. Manette's recurring mental illness represents the powerful grip his tortured past has upon him and distances him from direct responsibility for his actions. Yet his frequent delusions— for example, after he realizes that it is through his actions that the husband of his daughter has been condemned to die—can never be permanent. The loving attentions of a reunited Charles and Lucie, safe in England, will restore his health, and most importantly, his moral center. Just as in the case of his recovery after eighteen years' wrongful imprisonment in the Bastille, Dr. Manette will recover: not only because he has done no wrong, but because he knows how to forgive.

Madame Defarge: Madame Defarge is the character in *A Tale of Two Cities* who embodies a Revolution gone horribly wrong. Commanding respect and fear in equal measure, Madame Defarge is never softened (except just prior to her death) through any personal or endearing reference. Even her proud husband consistently retreats before her unbending will: "A great woman...a strong woman, a grand woman, a frightfully grand woman!" At once imposing mother, vengeful daughter, and monumental bride-in-waiting to the Revolution, Madame Defarge lives for nothing else, and cannot—will not—survive it. Like the excesses of Revolution itself, Madame Defarge is beyond help.

THOSE DEAD ARE MY DEAD, AND THAT SUMMONS TO ANSWER FOR THOSE THINGS DESCENDS TO ME!

It is in Madame DeFarge's knitting that the names of all of the enemies of the Revolution are "registered," a "shroud" destined for those to be punished in a Revolution that comes, increasingly, to resemble Madame DeFarge's *personal* "hit list". In her we see how revolutionary ideals can be corrupted by personal ambition and vengeance. Dickens would have us believe that Madame Defarge betrays not only Darnay and the Manettes, but also those ideals of the Revolution's first phase—many of which were modeled on the American revolution of 1776.

LETTRES DE CACHE

The story of Dr. Manette's imprisonment by the Marquis de Saint Evremonde is explained in *A Tale of Two Cities*. Not so clear is how he is imprisoned, and by whose authority. One of the worst abuses practiced among the ruling elite in France prior to 1789 was what in French is called the *Lettres de cachet* (translated literally as a writ or letter of distinction, it is also a pun on the French verb "cacher" which means "to hide"). Nobles like Saint Evremonde could have their personal and political enemies imprisoned indefinitely without trial or due process of law *solely on the basis of their accusation*. No firm proof was required by the corrupt agents of the monarchy who looked the other way when it came time for old grudges or differences to be settled. Darnay himself suggests in "The Gorgon's Head" (in Part Two) that his uncle would have so imprisoned him in an instant had he not

been out of favor in the French court.

Lettres de cachet were technically abolished by the revolutionary councils in 1789, although after reading Dickens's novel it should come as no surprise that newly freed citizens also used them even *after* the Revolution, often against their former masters. In 1776, American revolutionaries, too, abolished the English monarch's version of imprisonment without due process of law, the *writ of habeus corpus*. Not surprisingly, the right of citizens to a trial by their peers in a court of law, as well as the right to not be imprisoned for the same crime twice, were ultimately codified in the Constitutions of both the United States and France. Far from being automatic or "inalienable," these rights were first established, after tremendous struggle, in the time period Dickens represents in *A Tale of Two Cities*.

If one of the moral points of *A Tale of Two Cities* is that the sins of the father should not be visited upon the son, that Charles Darnay should not have to lose his head for the crimes of his tyrannical uncle, then Madame Defarge pays heavily for her devotion to excessive violence in the course of the Revolution. At the end of the novel, Charles Darnay is freed, while Madame Defarge is ultimately a victim of her own desire for revenge. In seeking the execution of the entire family of the Marquis Saint Evremonde (Darnay), including Lucie and her daughter, Madame Defarge goes outside any reasonable limits of the revolutionary plan. We accept that Madame Defarge has suffered under the old regime, but she is a dangerous character in the novel, lacking the desire to forgive, within reason, the crimes of others.

Charles Darnay. Darnay's role in the novel is to break away from France's corrupt aristocratic past. To this end, he gives up his uncle's title, that of the Marquis Saint Evremonde: "I would abandon [France] and live otherwise and elsewhere. It is little to relinquish. What is it but a wilderness of misery and ruin?" Darnay's right to a new beginning is a universal one that *A Tale of Two Cities* endorses strongly. And, of course, it is on English soil that Darnay will make his fresh start.

Darnay is, like Lucie, an ideal of human conduct asserting the right to a second chance in life despite prior associations. (It is interesting to note that Charles Darnay shares Dickens's initials; remember Dickens's own new beginning in 1859!)

Darnay is also a nobleman by birth, and his actions throughout the novel display French nobility of spirit supported by a strong dose of British individualism. Darnay helps the enfeebled Dr. Manette, is gentlemanly in his courtship of Lucie, and valiant in his own defense when held on trial for treason in both England and France. He is, however, the unflinchingly *good* character in the book, and his steady devotion to Lucie and all that is right lacks the convincing depth of Carton's character. Darnay is in the final analysis a little dull.

Sidney Carton. If Darnay represents the positive hope of reinvigorated human potential, Carton—his double and mirror-image—represents the falling-short, and failure of that ideal. Described as a "jackal" and scavenger of the dead, Carton is nevertheless a man of substantial, if wasted, talents. We suspect strongly that Carton is the true and unacknowledged genius behind the worldly success of his friend, the prominent and striving defense attorney, Mr. Stryver. Carton saves Darnay from the scaffold not once, but twice, in England and France. Yet Carton, like the box suggested by his name, is trapped in the world of "reality" and a fallen human nature. Carton's vision is a dark one, and he goes to his death willingly knowing that his hopes, through his sacrifice, will belong to Darnay.

Yet Carton is redeemed in *A Tale of Two Cities*, like Dr. Manette and Darnay, through the love of Lucie. Having acknowledged that he cannot

IN ENGLAND, DARNAY AND HIS WIFE LIVED HAPPILY. A DAUGHTER, LUCIE, WAS BORN, AND GREW.

NICE OF YOU TO VISIT, CARTON.

I CAME TO SEE MY LITTLE LUCIE.

win Lucie's love, Carton earns the affection of the Darnay family, most especially their children. And while Darnay may share Dickens's initials, most scholars agree that Carton, not Darnay, more closely recalls the energy and imagination of the writer. As such, Carton seems to be the most autobiographical character in the novel.

Through the love of Lucie, the two character opposites, Carton and Darnay (last names that also share Dickens's initials), ultimately are united in an idealized figure of love. Darnay is, at the novel's end, a transformed and redeemed Carton. The fallen, dissolute Carton has gone to the guillotine and been reborn in the unconscious figure —still wearing Carton's clothes—that rides to safety in the Manettes' carriage.

Miss Pross. Miss Pross has a small, but significant, part to play in the historical drama of *A Tale of Two Cities*: Lucie's devoted caregiver and surrogate-mother. But Miss Pross is also strangely masculine— Jarvis Lorry initially mistakes her for a man, and her aspect is "brawny." Dickens describes Miss Pross as "the "wild red woman," and her consistent association with

the color red suggests her fiery temperament, bound vigorously to the Manettes through incontestable bonds of love.

Miss Pross plays both mother and father roles to Lucie in the months of crisis while Darnay is held by the Revolutionary council in Paris. Nurturing and loyal, Miss Pross is also a physical force to be reckoned with when it comes to the defense of her dear "Ladybird," the final protector of the Manettes and Darnay as they flee Paris. If Madame Defarge is the embittered matriarch of a French Revolution gone wrong, Miss Pross is the virtuous and equally powerful symbol of middle-class values (although Miss Pross is herself clearly working-class). In one of the novel's concluding climaxes, Miss Pross and Madame Defarge battle to the death over the right to create a future based upon their respective working-class views. Miss Pross's view, rooted in unquestionable loyalty to her genteel mistress, is triumphant.

Jarvis Lorry. Like Miss Pross, Jarvis Lorry—lifetime employee of Tellson's Bank—is guardian spirit of the Manette-Darnay cause. It is Mr. Lorry who looks after Lucie's affairs as her ward and, after the discovery of her father, plays an active and

PROMISE ME THAT NOTHING WILL INFLUENCE YOU TO CHANGE YOUR MIND. YOU MUST DRIVE AWAY WHEN MY PLACE IS FILLED. SEVERAL LIVES DEPEND ON IT!

I WILL DO MY PART FAITHFULLY.

nurturing role in the affairs of the Manettes. A business-oriented, yet deeply feeling man, Lorry's favorite exclamation is "Courage! Business!" Fundamentally honest, Lorry can neither deceive nor lie, and like Miss Pross he seems strangely immune to the violence of the Revolution in Paris, where he travels frequently on bank business. We see him angry only once; perhaps not surprisingly it is against Sydney Carton, whose seemingly indifferent and casual attitudes offend Lorry's sense of decency. Of course, Lorry's world view is a simple one, and he, in time, comes to appreciate the fullness of Carton's humanity In fact, Carton and Lorry have much in common—they have lived the best parts of their life sacrificing for others.

Character. While extremely detailed in its characterizations, *A Tale of Two Cities* doesn't rely upon sketches of actual historical personalities dating from the French Revolution. In fact, only two events recounted in the novel, the storming of the Bastille, and the minor episode of the murder of the informant Foulon, have any direct relation to what actually happened. The result is that the plot of *A Tale of Two Cities* paints a vivid backdrop (Dickens's sense of everyday life in 18th century France) without depending on the "heroic" status of any of its characters. Of course, Carton's actions at the novel's end are heroic, but they are also those of an opportunistic character, a rather ordinary man of untested talents, upon whom history has forced great deeds. The novel suggests that revolution breeds heroes and heroines from likable common people, whom Dickens would have us believe (rather modestly) are basically good but all too easily misled.

Dickens on Revolution. Dickens's fascination with details and vivid descriptions of Revolution-era France is present everywhere in *A Tale of Two Cities*. For example, Dickens delights in relating the details of the revolutionary group in the St. Antoine quarter of Paris, that hotbed of "Jacques" (called in French history a "Jacquerie") out of which springs the beast known as the Parisian "mob." We are led to believe that code words, secret associations, and long-kept grudges are the explosive mixture that will ignite the slumbering passions recounted in Dickens's pages.

Yet Dickens never directly supports the revolutionaries' cause, although he continually focuses his powerful descriptions upon them, giving them an air of pity and even righteousness. For example, Dickens gives us the tale of the eccentric Gaspard, who first foreshad-

THAT NIGHT, AS THE MARQUIS SLEPT...

ows the violence to come by his writing the word "blood" on the pavement across from the Defarge's wine shop. It is Gaspard whose child is run over and killed by the Marquis's carriage and who achieves a remarkable, if desperate, revenge before himself going to the gallows.

So where does Dickens stand on the issue of Revolution? In a remarkable passage early on in the text which addresses 18th century society's tendency to glorify violence, Dickens states that: "the precept 'Whatever is is right,' an aphorism that would be as final as it is lazy, did not include the troublesome consequence that nothing that ever was, was wrong." Dickens seems to be saying that the French Revolution was a dangerous event, to be avoided at any cost, at the same time acknowledging that it was the perhaps inevitable consequence of a violent and destructive social system designed to bring out the worst in people. In Carton's case, on the other hand, the revolution brings out the best.

In the end, Dickens's position on revolution is a delicate and careful compromise. In political terms, Dickens didn't accept the idea of revolution on any other level than the personal (such as his own transformation in 1859). But this "personal" level of revolution and transformation is significant. Throughout *A Tale of Two Cities*, Dickens combines his fear of revolution with pity for the

urban poor who, like Gaspard (and perhaps even Madame Defarge) are forced to view revolution as their only alternative.

Personal Virtue. The unfolding of the plot of *A Tale of Two Cities* compares Dickens's view of the role of literature in society with the roles of faith, religion, or what the Victorians more regularly called "Providence." The novel, Dickens said, was but a "little imitation" of greater moral and religious principles.

The pervasive gloom and shadow that consistently falls over Carton and Dr. Manette, the Old Bailey and the Bastille, and all of revolutionary-era France, demands a moral response in literary form. Without it, France will remain the breeder of revolution, peopled with starving "scarecrows" in the fields and the "leprosy of unreality" at the French Court. For England's part, Carton—who describes himself, "I am like one who died young"— requires the love of something, of providence (or of providence embodied: Lucie Manette, described as "the Golden Thread"). Without it, Carton (and England) will remain undead and never be "recalled to life." *A Tale of Two Cities*, Dickens's "little imitation" of greater principles and faith, is in this light a good imitation; its plot offers to protect its readers from the sickness of personal despair as well as the full-blown disease of revolution.

Theme Analysis

Individual vs. Societal Rights. It is interesting that in *A Tale of Two Cities* the actions of a populace, a "mob," and an entire country are brought to bear on the lives of a few individuals. Weighing one's personal rights and liberties against the obligation to greater society was as pressing an issue in Dickens's day as at the time of the French Revolution. Dickens had criticized specific actions of British government during the British involvement in the Crimean war (against Russia) in 1855. At that time he had declared that his work attempted "to understand the heavier social grievances and to help set them right". We can easily tell that *A Tale of Two Cities* addresses social themes (and "grievances") directly, and brings them up to date in 1859 terms.

History or Romance? Dickens constantly measures the collective life of the French Revolution against individual romance and idealism, and the individual usually comes out on top. Carton's final action is an *individual's* choice about what is right, rather than a revolutionary set of ideas or values. This tension between revolutionary and romantic perspectives is one of the reasons why *A Tale of Two Cities* is often labeled an "historical romance." Not quite a completely fictional romance, and not really a history textbook, *A Tale of Two Cities* adapts the history of the French Revolution to suit its romantic needs.

One of the versions of romance that *A Tale of Two Cities* presents is the vision of history as a tragedy of the common man. Sidney Carton is one such everyman: he is depressed, drinks too much, and, but for the accident that he resembles Darnay, could be anyone. Through weight of chance, and the romanticized figure of his own destiny, Carton becomes a tragic (and romantic) hero —greater in death than he ever might have been in life.

Rebirth and Resurrection Dickens doesn't offer *A Tale of Two Cities* as merely romantic, however. Moral regeneration and resurrection, the theme of purity and the love of others, runs strongly through the novel. The plot begins with Jarvis Lorry, the agent of Tellson's Bank, going to "dig up," to rescue, Dr. Manette from a living death in a French prison after eighteen years of unjust imprisonment. In fact, the title of the entire first section is "Recalled to Life," and this theme persists throughout the novel: being recalled to a more virtuous path of action and conduct (a path Darnay embraces and Madame Defarge rejects); being recalled to an ultimate sacrifice for the love of others (Sidney Carton); being recalled to the actions of the past so that they may be addressed and remedied in the present through non-violent and peaceful means. A character not seen in the Classics Illustrated adaptation is Jerry Cruncher, a grave robber or "resurrection man." He, too, is recalled to a better life, but as a clown, a jester, and (despite once-soiled hands) a likable man. *A Tale of Two Cities* always presents tragic events in everyday life against the backdrop of redeeming possibilities and potentials.

The Absent Father. The theme of imprisonment of the body and spirit in *A Tale of Two Cities* is made all the more remarkable by the fact that it is primarily *fathers* who appear in prisons or are imprisoned. In fact, Dickens's obsession with fathers, prisons, and fathers in prisons appears in many of his works. Where fathers do appear, they are usually associated with injustice and delinquency (although not always of their own doing). The imprisoned father at the beginning of *A Tale of Two Cities* is Dr. Manette; at the conclusion it is Darnay himself. Issues of abandonment and delinquency also cast shadows on the actions of fathers in the novel. Dr. Manette does not tell his family about the writing of the letter against the original Marquis Saint Evremonde that caused his illegal imprisonment, a secrecy which up until his release ensures that his family, believing him dead, will never receive justice. Nor does Darnay consult with Lucie and her father concerning his actions when—for presumably noble reasons—he returns to France and exposes himself to danger for his former servant the postmaster Gabelle.

The "mob." *A Tale of Two Cities* marks Dickens's obsession, fascination, and ultimate disgust with mob violence. In many books, paintings, and articles of this Victorian period, the mob is a frightening and deadly image of discontent and unrest in the city.

The mob loses any individual responsibility or identity in *A Tale of Two Cities* except that of group anger and destruction. Without a name, the mob cannot be held accountable for the inexcusable crimes it commits in the name of justice. After the violence has passed, however, we read that the mob breaks down into its various parts:

> *Yet, human fellowship infused some nourishment into the flinty viands, and struck some parts of cheerfulness out of them. Fathers and mothers who had their full share in the worst of the day, played gently with their meager children; and lovers, with such a world around them, and before them, loved and hoped.*

The mob is made up of humans, after all, and Dickens's point is not to endorse its violence (he deplores it, in fact), but to ask the reader to address the forces that can change the "human fellowship" of good people into the fallen humanity and animal-like violence of the mob. Nor does Dickens play favorites: the mob and its horrible potential appear in *A Tale of Two Cities* in both England and France, the path of destruction, of innocent persons and property, being "the usual progress of a mob" regardless of national origin. Interestingly, the mob appears attending the treacheries of Robert Cly/John Barsad, the treacherous spy-for-hire, on *both* sides of the English Channel. So even if the motives and actions of the mob are suspicious, there is a strange justice in the appropriateness of some of its victims.

• What is significant about *A Tale of Two Cities* as a title? What about Dickens's other proposed titles (Memory Carton, The Golden Thread, etc.): to which events might each of these titles refer? Why do you think that Dickens rejected them and settled upon *A Tale of Two Cities*?

• The American Revolution in 1776 had a profound impact upon social and political affairs in France in the decade preceding the French Revolution in 1789 (see **A Timeline of the Revolution** above). The corrupt class of French noblemen embodied in the Marquis Saint Evremonde, actually *supported* the American revolutionaries against the English monarch, George III, after 1778. Little did "Monseigneur" realize that the winds of revolution would soon visit— disastrously—upon his own shores. 1) What were the debts the French philosophers and revolutionaries in 1789 had to the American Revolution? 2) How was the French Constitution modeled after the American Declaration of Independence? How was it different? 3) Should French aristocrats have realized that the principles they supported in America's revolution would mean the ultimate downfall of their own society?

• In *A Tale of Two Cities*, Madame Defarge represents the problem of having too much memory and not enough forgiveness, not only at an individual level, but for French society in general. She is the person who, machine-like, "registers" crimes in her knitting. Her charac-ter, which Dickens alternately describes as seeing nothing and everything, is the absolute and unflinching *witness* of the events that unfold prior to the storming of the Bastille fortress. 1) What other witnesses can you identify—both sympathetic and unsympathetic—in *A Tale of Two Cities*? Are we, the readers, sympathetic or unsympathetic witnesses? Is Dickens?

• Identify and make a list of all of the pairings or doubles you can locate in *A Tale of Two Cities*. As examples, recall that England is measured against France, the healthy Doctor Manette against the mentally ill Doctor Manette and, of course, Carton against Darnay. Even Darnay's father and uncle were twins. Ideas and images (for instance, blood and wine, rainfall and footfall) are also associated descriptively in the novel. Why does Dickens use character and image pairings or "doubles" in *A Tale of Two Cities*, and how do you think they are useful?

THE ESSAYIST

Stuart Christie is a doctoral candidate at the University of California at Santa Cruz, where he is affiliated with The Dickens Project, a national consortium of sixteen colleges and universities that focuses on the works of Charles Dickens.